Weddings and Witchcraft

ANDI R. CHRISTOPHER

A catalogue record for this book is available from the National Library of New Zealand.

ISBN

978-0-473-70666-1 (paperback)

978-0-473-70667-8 / 978-0-473-70668-5 (ebook)

Weddings and Witchcraft

Laurel Windflower stepped forward and opened her eyes. The mirror showed the person she recognised, and someone else entirely. Same Laurel, same pinched nose and pale skin, same blue hair – though her roots needed doing, she noted. But the dress...

She spun round to look at her mother, perched on a chair by the window.

"What do you think?"

"What do *you* think, dear? It's your dress."

Laurel knew full well her mother had a *lot* of opinions about her youngest child's upcoming wedding and was doing very well at keeping a lid on most of them. She gnawed on her lower lip and took another look. White, not ridiculously long, with lace at the top but not too fancy, well fitted – if with pins for now – it checked all the boxes. But there was more...

"I... I didn't expect to love it," she said, finding herself ridiculously almost in tears. She didn't even believe in marriage that much. And yet... She took another look.

"Is it within budget?" she asked, cautiously. Her mother assured her it was. Laurel pretended she didn't hear the numbers. She couldn't imagine paying that much for one item of clothing and if it had been left to her she wouldn't have. She'd been reluctant to accept it from her mother until her father had taken her aside and made it clear that they were enjoying every bit of this and the money was well spent on them as well.

The shop owner was *delighted*, trilling about how beautiful Laurel would look, and what a fashionable choice she'd made. Laurel's mother basked in that conversation too, even as Laurel was starting to find it a bit overwhelming. This is done, she'd told herself, going through the endless checklists that seemed to be implanted in her head as well as on her phone and on a giant corkboard in their apartment. Venue, date, celebrant, and now dress – and they were checking out caterers while her mother was here as well – those were the main things, but it still seemed like every item ticked off was like a hydra head, spawning several more.

And that was without even thinking about the logistics of moving to Sweden on top of it all.

Laurel rubbed her eyes and forced herself to pay attention, to agree to the dates for alterations and confirm the details, her mother putting a deposit on her card. They headed outside and turned to head in the direction of the car...

...and then it caught Laurel, all at once, the intoxicating smell of dried elder leaves starting to burn, mixed with the scent of larkspur flowers, and something else she couldn't quite identify. The world started to tilt around her and her knees buckled, the ground racing up towards her at an alarming pace. She was only saved by her mother catching her under the arms at just the right moment and lowering her gently down to sit on the edge of the footpath, her feet in her gutter.

So much for the dignity of dress buying.

The shop owner came running out.

"No breakfast this morning, is it? Try and at least have some tea with honey or something, love. I know you want to look your best for the big day, but you don't want to be collapsing."

Laurel blinked at her.

"You think I'm dieting because I'm getting married? Do people really do that?"

The shop owner flushed. "Uh, most brides, if I'm honest, try and lose a bit. I tell everyone they're beautiful as they are – because everyone is beautiful on their special day – but we still assume our alterations will need to account for losing a bit. But, uh..."

"They're having to plan the wedding in quite a rush," Laurel's mother explained.

"Oh my dear, of course. No wonder you're feeling a bit woozy. Congratulations though."

"NO!" Laurel almost yelled. "Oh my God, no, I'm not pregnant."

"They're moving to Europe two weeks after," her mother said knowingly, thankfully saving her from who knew what other terrible scenario for her body. "I think she just needs a lie-down and maybe some sugar."

Laurel was relieved to make it to the car in one piece and slumped onto the passenger seat.

"Did you smell anything?" she asked. "When we left the shop, did you smell anything?"

"I hope you're not," was the reply, "starving yourself. You know that does damage in the long run, right?"

"Jesus Christ," muttered Laurel, winding down the car window and leaning back as the car left the central city and headed uphill into the suburbs. Her mother pretended she didn't hear.

Marigold Nightfield blinked herself awake after just a couple of hours of sleep. Spells for good will and for people to get along were, her research told her, among the easiest of spells when people wanted to, and the hardest when they were determined not to. She clambered out of bed, whispering to Laurel that she'd be back soon. She pulled on track pants and a t-shirt, grabbed the bag she'd put together earlier, and quietly headed outside, in time to make it to a little bit of public space suitable for carrying out a spell at midnight.

Marigold cleared the area on the grass, making sure nothing would catch alight, before lighting the yellow candle. She passed the malachite over it three times, speaking the spell out loud, and raised the candle up, seeking blessings.

When she extinguished the candle, she was calmer. Laurel's family had welcomed her. Her parents loved Laurel. There was goodwill enough there, but she wanted to prevent misunderstandings, one person reading another as cold, another taking offence at a turn of phrase, one being effusive and the other formal to the point of curt. The sort of thing she was all too familiar with.

It was an easy spell to do, she told herself, as she headed back home. An easy spell, and a load off her mind.

Laurel said goodbye to Marigold from brunch, who was heading up the hill to teach a class. As soon as she had gone, Laurel's mother decided it was shoe-shopping time. At this point, Laurel just wanted to wear her sneakers and be done with it, but she knew there wasn't much point in arguing. Then the following day they were meeting two potential caterers and she and Marigold had a cake tasting the following week – she was dragging Marigold, who claimed all cake was good cake, because she didn't want to have to make a single decision all on her own. They also had to confirm their visas and temporary accommodation and...

"Florists," Laurel's mother said. "Don't forget florists."

"Oh, we're handling that ourselves. We don't need much, given the venue."

"You need to make sure you have nice bouquets... oh no, will Connor want to carry a bouquet. What about Sorrel? They won't be into that sort of thing – or maybe they will now they're dressing more feminine. Oh no, why must everything be so complicated these days?"

Laurel paused and looked at her mother, standing outside the shoe shop in the pedestrianised street, looking completely bewildered at the modern world. Laurel – who had half-heartedly considered getting a celebrant in Marigold's back garden and ordering pizza for everyone – was very tempted to throw it back at her mother: why *was* it all so complicated? Why did she *need* shoes? But she looked up at her mother and remembered that she actually really liked the perfect white dress she had tried on yesterday, and decided to let it go.

"There's another shoe shop just along here," she said, ushering her mother. "Don't worry, we've got the flowers all sorted, it's going to look perfect."

In the next shop, they found shoes. Laurel was unused to heels and not going to start now – besides, she added, she was already taller than Marigold so it didn't make sense to add any more height on. Fortunately, her mother agreed and they ended up with a very nice – and not too expensive – pair of white ballet flats which met her needs just fine. Laurel visualised moving another few Post-its over and felt her shoulders already beginning to relax. This was doable. An end was in sight.

"You know, Laurel," her mother said. "I know you're not very traditional, and I love that about you." Laurel paused to think about if 'not very traditional' meant gay or blue-haired. It couldn't mean she was a witch, because that was most of her family. Then again, most of her family was turning out to be queer as well. Must be the blue hair. But she didn't say anything. "But I'm so glad you went for a traditional dress, even if it doesn't have all the frills. Because you look incredible."

Laurel decided to not interpret it as a backhanded compliment and just bask in the idea. Her mother could be A Lot and this wedding wasn't entirely bringing out the best in her but Laurel still didn't know what she'd do without her. She hadn't quite realised what alien territory weddings were.

"Marigold's been making some information sheets," she told her mother. "Just what's on our website, but I know the older people won't all see that, and the invites went out in such a hurry they only had the basics on. We were thinking of including some dried flowers or maybe some lavender – because that's part of our theme – you know those little sachets you put with our clothes and stuff. Sort of as advance guest favours, and because everyone likes getting things in the post, don't they?"

The question worked. Laurel had given her mother something else but her appearance to have opinions about, and she sank back in the passenger seat with a smile while her mother considered how flat a sachet would have to be for postage to be charged at the letter rate.

Marigold stood in the garden in front of her father's house. For all the time she'd been back in Wellington – even after she'd moved out of the house – she'd maintained this garden, with its little paths and carefully organised beds, all in straight lines. It had been her grandmother's – her grandmother who had also lived here in the last years of her life – and then it had become a resource for many witches of the city, especially those newly arrived, starting their own gardens in pots on the windowsills and decks of rented houses. There were people who would help maintain it in her absence – her father didn't have the talent, but he'd keep it watered and others would do the more difficult work. But things were feeling so impermanent. Her father wouldn't keep the big house forever – he'd shown no interest in future relationships, and would most likely be downsizing before too long.

It felt like she could prolong things a few years, but she was only putting off its inevitable destruction.

Marigold stretched up from where she had been kneeling on a cushion, placed her secateurs gently down. She snapped her fingers and cast a light glowing on her hands. It burned as well as ever, soft and warm, glowing in front of her face. She wasn't sure what to do about it. Her magic powers had shown no significant sign of fading.

Initially, she'd tried learning all she could, aware that her time was limited, taking the most of this opportunity to have real experience of magic rather than just studying it on a theoretical level. Now... now she didn't know what to do. It seemed a waste to do any more of it, but she couldn't put all her energy into something that was going to disappear at any moment.

Here she was: magic, and on the brink of a new life! Her PhD complete, a wedding and an international move looming. She didn't need magic for any of those but it felt intertwined with all of them, as if it was running through her veins and connecting her to everything.

She could do without the powers. There were plenty of other things she was more than capable of doing. But the sensation of having magic, the feeling of belonging and being connected, that was something that it was going to be hard to lose.

No time for angst, she told herself, getting back to the rest of the weeding and pruning, checking her list of things she needed to bring back to the apartment. She was cooking tonight as well, and Laurel's mother was in town, and there was *so much* in her life she needed to get sorted that she needed to focus. She pushed herself to get it together, finished the rest of her work, said goodbye to her father, and caught the bus back most of the way into town with a paper bag full of herb cuttings. From there she walked up the hill to the small block of flats in which she and Laurel were living, stopping at the nearby sushi shop to see what she could find reduced at the end of the day. She wasn't in the mood for cooking and if she could find a way out of it that way then she was sure as hell going to take it.

While she was paying, she saw something creeping out of the backroom door. Yellow fur, a claw that seemed more talon than something you'd find on a mammal.

"Oh, you have a monster?" she asked, sunnily.

The tall Korean woman behind the counter looked stricken, yelling something and motioning away. The claw disappeared.

"My son... my son, he plays dress up, I'm so sorry!" she said frantically struggling to get the words out.

"Oh, it's no problem. I'm used to monsters. If you ever need any help...?"

"No. Thank you! Have a great evening!"

Marigold took that as her cue to leave and, slightly disappointed at not having met the monster, she headed home where Laurel was, as she should have expected, in wedding planning chaos.

Laurel carefully moved the "Laurel's outfit" Post-it to the In Progress part of the corkboard. Her mother had gone off to see an old friend. She supposed she should take a lie down, but it seemed such a waste of time when there was so much work to do. She jabbed at the board with her finger: cake, caterers, attendant outfits – she needed to talk to Sorrel again about that.

The other corkboard had a Swedish flag pinned on the top, and most of that was still at the To-Do stage. She'd understood a while ago that Marigold's career would mean some time overseas, and she was excited for that, but the timing wasn't ideal, now her business was going so well. Still, she'd made some contingency plans, and when this was all over, when all the organising was done and they were finally on a plane, she was looking forward to it. A new city, the chance to learn a new language, weekend trips around Europe...

She was interrupted by a soft scratching sound behind her.

"Hey Tibbs," she said, but it didn't seem to be Tibbs, who was likely out exploring, as he tended to – oh God and getting Tibbs to Sweden was an adventure in itself. No, because under the door she saw an envelope. Definitely unusual – there'd be no reason to bring it here rather than putting it in the box. She opened it and found only plant matter.

Elder leaves, so dry they could break in her hands. Pressed and dried larkspur. And this was the one she'd had trouble identifying – fresh cut willow, English willow, those tall, pencil-like trees, rather than the weeping Japanese sort. Their scent was warm and fresh, green willow they called it.

The same plants she'd smelled before she collapsed.

Fortunately smelling them like this was not enough for her to feel anything more than very briefly woozy. She put them back in the envelope and turned it over, looking for an address, handwriting, any sign of where or who it came from. Finding nothing, she headed outside to try and see if she could see who'd delivered them. The door to the corridor off which their apartment and two others were placed was propped open – building management didn't like it, but everyone did it, and it had never really concerned Laurel before.

There was no-one. She looked up and down the hill. A couple of cars went by but they didn't seem to have been coming from her place, and no-one was obviously walking away either.

There was nothing.

This really isn't the time for mysteries, Laurel said to herself, putting the envelope on top of a bookcase and plugging in her headphones to make sure she met her daily Duolingo target and didn't provoke the owl. She was making dinner that night, and she supposed it was almost time to prep. A nice, quiet, ordinary life with a bit of magic – that was what Laurel Windflower wanted.

And no weird deliveries of plants were going to stand in the way of that.

Marigold had no idea where the envelope came from either, but she had picked up two helpings of discounted teriyaki chicken and rice from the sushi shop before it closed.

"One more thing solved!" Laurel said. "Dinner!"

"Mmm yes. I'm going to heat up the garlic bread from yesterday as well, you want some?"

"What a combination... sure, why not."

Marigold stared at the kitchen for a moment. They'd never intended to stay in this apartment long, and it hadn't become home in the way other places had been. But it had been the first place they'd lived together, and it still seemed strange how soon they'd be leaving it all behind. She turned back to Laurel.

"I got the stuff you needed as well. Also, I need to go through the cupboards and find things we don't use often so we can try to use them up. I know it's still a couple of months before we leave, but some of this stuff it's only a tiny amount every time I bake or something, and I hate having it go to waste."

"I wouldn't worry too much," Laurel said. "Connor will eat just about anything and we can box it up for him on the last day. Charity for the hard-up start-up folk."

"He'll *eat* just about anything. Doesn't mean he knows how to cook with anything. Good luck if you're planning to hand him a half-used tub of cream of tartar and a jar of capers."

"He might surprise you!" Laurel said optimistically.

"Hmm. Where are our herbs going? And not Connor, he'd kill them in a day."

Laurel looked out to the collection of herbs in pots which almost filled the balcony. It wasn't a huge collection – nothing to compare with what Marigold's grandmother had created, for example, but some of them had been hers since she started uni – they'd been with her a long time and even though she knew she'd quite easily build up a collection of replacements in Sweden, she'd still miss them.

"Nah, don't worry. The shop's going to take them, sell the more obscure ones, and give away the more common ones to baby witches or people new to the city."

Marigold looked at Laurel and felt pride welling inside her.

"You really have thought of everything, haven't you."

Laurel sat down on the sofa, spread her arms and threw herself backwards.

"I'm scared of what I haven't thought of. That I've missed something really obvious that everyone just assumes you know about."

"That sounds way too like one of my worries. You know we're not meant to share them."

"That's not one of the features of getting married?"

"Ha! If it is we're most of the way there already." Marigold said. "If only. If only."

After two hours of teaching, Marigold headed down into Hataitai, a coastal suburb just to the east of the city centre. She walked down the hill and caught the bus from town. This was her main task for the week, and she needed to make sure she was on time. She found herself oddly tight of breath as she boarded the bus – there was so much to do before the wedding, but she also had time to do it in, and the combination of pressure without enough motivation to speed her up made her uneasy.

For the first time, Marigold was working the equivalent of one regular full-time job, rather than three. She taught a few labs at uni which gave her enough to pay her share of the rent, and she had her own research projects, particularly the one on monsters, the one that had brought her to Laurel's front door all those years ago. But, for the first time she could remember, there was almost space in her life for... not doing much.

Or at least there would be if she didn't have to plan a wedding on top of it all.

Still, she was making the most of it, sitting people-watching in cafes, walking up over the greenbelt that surrounded the city, and watching the harbour from new vantage points. Even if she was only going to be gone for a couple of years, she would miss this city, never truly feel at home elsewhere.

The ride to Hataitai was just a short one, though the other side of the bus tunnel and down to the little collection of shops and takeaways that formed the suburb centre. Marigold got off just before the main shopping area and walked up the hill. She checked her map even though she'd been here before, and a small sign on the mailbox confirmed she had the right place. The Villa was painted a sort of old-fashioned pale yellow, which at once blended in and yet, impossibly, stood out from its surroundings. The studio was cosy, with just a little curtained space to get changed, a couple of seats, some dressmakers' dummy and various samples of fabric and thread and other assorted needs they had between them that were now being met.

Sadie opened the door and showed Marigold through to her workshop in the front room, looking over the dress Marigold had brought in as requested, running the fabric through her fingers, taking in the shape and composition.

Marigold stood in the changing area, taking deep breaths and convincing herself that this was all going to work. She was trying on not her own dress but a few samples the dressmaker had made – she said that alongside measurements they helped her work out exactly how things would go on a real body, not just the fit but things like how the fabric draped.

Marigold was only too happy to have someone else understand this all for a change.

Laurel was being excellent at shouldering the work of planning, she really was. She was the one with the spreadsheet and the budget, and Marigold mostly just had to be where she was needed – cake tasting! Venue walkthrough!

– and make decisions. She was trying to do that well at least – her instinct was always to throw questions back to the asker, but she had learned that was less than helpful. There was one thing she did have to sort out for herself.

And that was what she was going to wear.

Wedding dress codes were, ugh, so binary. It felt like whatever you chose was making a statement. And Marigold... she didn't feel right in a traditional dress, but a tux would be making a much more masculine statement than she felt. They'd had a whole discussion about Sorrel being in the wedding party, and a waistcoat worked for them but for Marigold...

...no wedding fair or dress designer was going to be able to handle this for her. Marigold was going to have to handle this herself.

With a little help, of course.

"...you're going to have to pull it apart, aren't you?"

Sadie turned the dress inside our and ran her fingers along the seams.

"No, I don't think so. No, I can trace these pieces and just add an extra margin, and then I'll get you in for a fitting just to make sure it's exactly right for you. I assume you want to keep the pockets?"

"Hell yeah, all the pockets! Weddings seem to be full of stuff so I'll want to keep my phone and my multitool on me if nothing else."

Sadie laughed a little uncomfortably. "You know, most people would be thinking of tissues and their lipstick to touch up, but both of those sound useful. Right."

Sadie put Marigold's dress in a brown bag and wrote her name and a date on it. She then pushed it to one side.

"Okay, so you just want cotton for the main dress. I'll let you go buy that. I'll write down what you need for the shop. Don't tell them it's a wedding dress or they'll freak."

"Not typical wedding dress material then?"

"It's not shiny or lacy so I'd give that a no. They'll talk you into something you don't want and then charge you three times as much just because it's for a wedding. Let me just work out how much I need – I may need to go a bit over because I can't tell until I make the pattern exactly how much it will take... is that okay?"

"Sure."

In Marigold's head was pretty much the perfect outfit for her. She just needed to see if she could pull it off.

Sadie took measurements around her chest and waist and neck, and down her spine, scribbling them into a notebook alongside little diagrams.

It was unorthodox, but the dressmaker only asked if she was sure a total of three times, which is what she would have expected from anyone, and didn't seem overly sceptical of her plans. And honestly, it was more traditional than a lot of people who knew her would have expected. She was wearing a dress, for heaven's sake! She was even wearing white, mostly.

Mostly.

"And you'll bring me the ribbon when you have it?"

Marigold nodded enthusiastically. "It's en route from Turkey, of all places. I've got it tracked so it probably won't take too long to get here."

"Excellent! I look forward to seeing it. And your partner has her dress all sorted."

"Yup, though she's not showing me. She's going much more traditional – like, actually got it from a bridal shop – but not too over the top, from what I understand. Her mother described it as 'modern', though not in a *very* disparaging way."

"Hah! In-laws. The most fun part of being married."

Marigold shrugged.

"I like Laurel's family. But I also like that we're going to be overseas for a while. Get a chance to do things on our own terms."

"That makes sense. Sort of an extended honeymoon."

"A honeymoon with a lot of work involved," Marigold responded, "but yes. I'll get that fabric, maybe Thursday if that's okay."

Laurel felt bad for feeling relieved when her mother finally headed home. She knew she would miss her when they went to Sweden – even though her parents were talking about visiting at some point – but right now everything was too much. She still had to take Tibbs to the vet for a second round of injections. She never worried about having him vaccinated before, because he was, after all, a familiar and not a regular cat, and already well past the record age for the latter.

Worse, as well as making up some story about him being a rescue from a former flatmate to avoid detailing the fact that he was now in his late twenties, actively impossible for a cat, she was going to have to take him in a carrier. There was a good chance he would never forgive her. But her walking there with him alongside her had raised a lot of suspicions, and she was relying on the vet to give her the paperwork she needed so he didn't have to languish in quarantine.

Admittedly she had no doubt he would quickly make his own way out of quarantine, but it was far easier to do this by the book. She did *not* want to have to contend with an escaping familiar in a new country, of all things.

Before Laurel even got to dealing with that, there were some things she had to look up. Larkspur and green willow and elderleaf, the herbs she smelled when she collapsed outside the dress shop and found again in that anonymous letter. She'd Googled them, of course, and found the usual range of uses, from culinary to the never-ending lists of spells for protection or good luck, but she had a sense there was something more going on and wanted to check the family spell book. It had been digitised so every family member could have a copy, but just as images, one giant PDF. She understood someone was actually making it fully searchable, which would be a dream, but today she still had to go through it page by page.

Fortunately, she was familiar with it enough to go through fairly quicky, not having to read every word. Some of the handwriting was a nightmare but at least she was used to it. There were people in her family who knew it much better than she did, as well as having a lot of background knowledge, and normally she would have asked for help, put her request out onto the witch chat – the somewhat chaotic, but always-loving-of-a-good-mystery network of witches and others with an interest in magic in her family. This time, though, she was hesitant. She had so little idea what was going on or who might be involved that she wanted to keep it to herself for now.

Plus the amount her family had been fussing over her had been A Lot lately, and she wasn't sure she wanted to subject herself to more of that.

Laurel lay down on her bed with her laptop and scrolled through page after page of the book. Once a plain hard-backed book with spells, recipes, and other notes it had been annotated and added to over the years, not only with comments and sketches, but with extra pages and clippings added in. Which meant whoever had scanned this had certainly had a job to do, and she was thankful for it. Even though she'd read every word of it, she still felt like she was coming to it anew, having context to make sense of things she didn't before, or being able to relate things to experiences that she'd had more recently. She found a reference to elder in a spell to aid sleeping, and one to larkspur in a spell to, of all things, ease milking in an older cow. Not all of this was written for the modern, urban context, evidently.

But she got to half way, finding no significant references to any of them and certainly not to them altogether. Her eyes were going blurry. She shut the lid of the laptop, stretched herself up, and headed through to the living room of their one-bedroom apartment.

This place hadn't exactly been home in the way her Aro Valley flat had. It had always felt a bit temporary, as if they'd paused from buying much furniture or much of anything, as it had always been the unspoken assumption, even before Marigold got awarded her postdoc, that they wouldn't be here very long. Still, even if it lacked some character and some sense of home, the warmth and dryness more than made up for it. No more having to clean black mould off the walls with bleach. It even saw the sun, through big windows that gave a fantastic view over the city. She was far from complaining. This, however temporary, was a good place for them both.

She was interrupted by Tibbs giving an almighty screech and hurling himself towards the front door.

"What in the...?" Tibbs did have his cat quirks, for certain, but he was on the whole better at dealing with things like a courier at the door than a regular cat. And there was certainly no need for outbursts like that. Laurel opened the door. There was no-one there. She looked down to find a small bouquet of herbs. Without picking it up she ran down the fire escape and out onto the road. No-one. Not even a car pulling out nor the sound of footsteps. They'd got away again.

Dismayed and frustrated, Laurel got herself back and picked up the bouquet. As she had guessed, it was mostly green willow and larkspur, though there was some lavender in there too.

And with them, a handwritten piece of card which read, in its entirety, *family*.

Laurel's hands shook as she half placed, half dropped, the bouquet onto the kitchen bench. What the hell was going on? She and Marigold had been so worried about forgetting someone important, so careful, going through social media and old emails and talking with family – and it was true they couldn't invite every acquaintance, and it was even true that they might have missed someone important by accident, and if so she could understand them feeling hurt by it. But this?

This was creepy as shit. Stalkery. Wrong.

Laurel made herself a cup of tea to try and calm down, bringing her laptop through into the lounge room to keep looking through the spell book. She still felt herself trembling even as she once again started scanning through the pages, hoping the sage and star anise tea would help her calm down a bit soon, trying not to be distracted by thinking about who she might have missed.

She was so distracted that she almost missed the reference to larkspur. To be fair, it was far from the clearest reference, scribbled up there in the corner, but it was there just the same. The name, a tiny sketch of the flowers, and the notes. Forgetfulness. Self-deception. Keeping secrets.

Laurel put her cup of tea down on the table. Her eyes grew wide.

Laurel had been sure her grandmother would have some insight on the question of Marigold being a witch, so she lingered at the end of the family video call until it was just her and Gran, and then she dragged Marigold in. Fortunately, Laurel's instincts had been correct. It should have surprised them to find out that Laurel's gran had no time for this sort of nonsense, but it was a relief all the same.

"Witches, not witches. Hereditary, not hereditary. All some modern oversimplification by those of you who think there's a witch gene, like there's a colour blindness gene or a cystic fibrosis gene. You think there's a witch gene or a witch protein, bah. Not that simple."

Marigold began to say that actually there was more than one possible cystic fibrosis gene, but forced herself to stick to the spirit of the point Laurel's grandmother was making. "Or like everyone has XX or XY chromosomes and those determine gender," Marigold said, and then paused, wondering if she'd pushed something that was going to break.

"Well exactly. There's all sorts in the spectrum of humanity. We like dividing things up into boxes, but there's always a lot more nuance than that accounts for. There are kids adopted into witching families who become witches. Sure biology is part of it, but so is who you grow up around. So is family. So are things we'll never be able to pinpoint. And as for being witches or not. Laurel, can you sing."

"Uh, not very well."

"Exactly. Very few people are amazing singers. Very few cannot sing at all. A lot of us can sing weakly or badly. Some can sing well. Some struggle with solos but do well in a choir. Get it?"

"I think so. Though I'm not quite sure how Marigold fits into this."

"Right, well, there are people who can tip the balance in a potion but nothing else. There are others who find the ability to save someone under extreme pressure, but can't use their powers in normal circumstances. There are children whose powers fade as they head for adulthood and others, especially in non-witching families, who only find them in adulthood. So yes, Laurel's a witch, and some people are not, but it doesn't mean everyone's so neatly classified."

"I think," Marigold said later that day, "that what I'm learning is there's a lot of established wisdom about witch-craft that is handed down through the generations, that's never actually been verified."

"No," Laurel said.

"No? You don't think that's the case?"

"No, you're probably right. I mean, no you do not have time to be creating and falsifying hypotheses about every aspect of magic since the beginning of time."

"Okay. Well, maybe I won't now. But I think we should just keep it in mind, you know. Not just assume things are true because everyone has always believed them and because they seem to make sense. It's a good starting point, but if something doesn't appear to add up investigating the established assumptions is a good thing. Right?"

"Right?" Laurel said, agreeing in theory but also a little concerned as to what Marigold Nightfield would get herself up to next.

Connor came round for dinner that evening, a not unusual occurrence, though Laurel admitted he was much more competent at not only cooking, but also having edible ingredients than he used to be. Things seemed to be going better for him too; he'd finally got his business in some kind of start-up incubator that was paying him and his colleagues for six months while they got it off the ground. Laurel just hoped it would last.

"Question for you," Laurel said hopefully. "If you had an eighty percent-full jar of cream of tartar, what would you use it for?"

Connor shifted on the edge of the armchair, well aware that Tibbs clearly had priority to the seat and was showing no signs of shifting or otherwise cooperating. He appeared to think for a few moments before responding.

"Oh, oh, is this that stuff you mix with Coke and it explodes?"

Laurel gave Marigold a knowing, if somewhat despairing, look.

"You're not going to tell me what on earth this is about, are you."

"Just baking..." Marigold said, looking outside the window.

"Okay just a question for you then," Connor said, very used to this sort of thing by now. "I was looking at the venue website and they say the lawn is suitable for a maximum of 50 people."

"They do say that," Laurel replied, grinning. "But we can fit more on than that."

"And you won't get into trouble?"

"Oh, they'll only see about fifty or so, and they won't be interested in enforcing rules when they see how lovely we are."

"You're going to mind control them?"

"Absolutely not! Just a little suggestibility. We're going to be careful, we'll clean up after ourselves and take care of the place, so a few extra relatives would do no harm."

Connor nodded, only rolling his eyes slightly. He was used to this stuff by now. He looked at his phone again.

"They also say there's no indoor alternative. Isn't that a bit risky with Wellington's weather being what it is?"

Laurel laughed.

"Okay, controlling the weather isn't as easy as some people think, that's true. But with a whole crowd, more than half of them witches, you really don't think we're confident in holding off the rain for an hour or so."

"Right, yes. You're solving everything by magic."

"Oh God, if only. If only magic could choose a caterer for us. Or do dress alterations... actually, that might work, but we've already signed a contract with the dressmaker for those. It helps, magic helps, but it doesn't solve all my problems, believe me."

"You still just want me to get a suit?"

"Yup. Any plain dark suit, it's only you in a suit so you don't need to match that. I've got this purple fabric in mind that I'm planning to use for a dress for Marigold's friend, a waistcoat for Sorrel, and a tie and pocket square for you. So you're all going to be neatly matched, *cohesive,* I think is the word, without needing to get something specially for the wedding."

"I would wear a dress for you if you wanted," Connor said.

"I know. But it's my wedding and I don't want you taking all the limelight, being the centre of attention."

"I hear you. I'll hide in the bush with a fern in front of my face."

Laurel chucked a small candle at his head, which he caught with one hand.

"Seriously though, Laurel, you getting married and us both all being respectable and having our own businesses. Who'da thought it."

"I know. I was thinking of sending some artfully cropped photos to the old crowd from school and letting them think we did end up together after all those years."

Laurel sipped her tea as Connor laughed. It had been years since she'd moved, and that within the same country – now she was heading to Sweden, and she'd have to meet new people, no longer be able to rely on the security of old friends. She hoped the balance in her mind would tip from intimidating to exciting sometime soon. Logically, she was pleased to be going, looking forward to it, but all the details of getting there – and the familiarity she'd be leaving behind – sometimes felt like it was altogether too much.

While Laurel was out shopping. Marigold sat cross-legged on the living room floor practising magic. She'd pushed out the furniture that moved easily – the armchair, the office chair at the little study desk she'd set up for herself at the window – not because magic needed space, not exactly, but because thinking did. Even though she didn't plan to move much, things not being too cluttered, and having the knowledge that she could, if she chose, lie back and stretch out every one of her limbs in all directions made her feel less constrained. It made her feel like there were more possibilities.

And magic was all about possibilities.

Marigold had linked a few basics – actions that didn't rely on tools or potions or anything beyond her own body or mind – together into a sort of warm-up routine. She went through them now, one after another, summoning her focus. She used her fingers to make a light, a glow that hung there like a flame. Then she spread her arms out into a circle and it hung there like a lens magnifying everything in front of her, out through the windows – it all came closer. When she turned her head the lens moved to stay in her direct vision. She shifted the degree of magnification back and forward a little, far away trees becoming closer, then further away, then closer again.

The third exercise also affected the senses, but this time sound, not vision. She created a mental volume button and by adapting it she could hear things outside that she shouldn't have been able to hear. It had limits, of course, but it wasn't just a matter of magnifying the sound ways that had already reached the house and bringing them into the range of Marigold's hearing, no it was a whole different kind of hearing, not just an enhanced version of her own. She took a deep breath in and out. Even these basic forms of magic had been hard won, but by now the routine had come together very well.

Marigold Nightfield was from a witching family – several in fact – but with no power of her own. Inevitably, though, she had access to a lot of information from a young age and was interested not just in the discovery of information but in the organisation and cataloguing of it as well; it was more than inevitable that she would become deeply involved in that area of magic. She learned some things herself, too – it was already established that wizards, unlike witches, did not require innate magical ability, and while most of their learning was simply about magic, most of them did end up able to practice simple magic, carry out a few spells, that sort of thing.

That was until last year. Last year everything had changed.

Laurel had found a metal object with the powers of a witch inside, hidden by Marigold's grandmother. Laurel had taken on the powers of one of Marigold's ancestors, and Marigold had developed the powers of a junior witch. She'd known, almost right from the start, that it wasn't going to be permanent, but neither she nor Laurel had been able to put their fingers on whether it would leave all at once or gradually dissipate. It had presented quite the challenge for Marigold who was unsure whether to put much focus on learning to use her abilities, knowing that it would disappear at some point and it would be such a waste, especially when she had such limited time and resources already. Alternatively, if she ignored it – well, she had one chance of being able to use magic, of being an actual witch! So few people got the opportunity! And it was even more significant for her because her mother had been a witch, her grandmother had been a witch, and it didn't help that some of the people who were most important to Marigold had some sort of magical ability either.

She had tried to tread a middle path which wasn't in her nature at all. She was used to all-in deep dives, obsessions as her father called them, as if he hadn't been going on about cantilevers and brise-soleils solidly for the entirety of Marigold's life. So she'd tried to develop her magic, but not at the expense of everything else she had going on in her life. She told herself to focus on the sort of learning that would be helpful for her in researching things about and relating to magic, experiences that would still be relevant even when she was no longer able to perform magic. But she hated the not knowing. Not knowing how fast or slow this ability would leave her. She hated not being able to plan for things, the idea she knew her life was going to change but not when or how.

For now, though, she did have her magic and she had her routine. She took a deep breath and moved on to the last of her five exercises.

Laurel was woken the next morning by Marigold's voice from the other room. Light was already streaming through the thin curtains, but the bed felt comfortably warm.

"What?" she called, reluctant to wake up.

"The information sheets?"

"On top of the bookcase by the window!"

"Yeah I know I..." Marigold appeared at the door of the room with a pile of paper in her hand, the information she had been putting together to send to guests, especially those with limited internet. "Did you spill... tea... or something on them?"

"What no?" Laurel reluctantly forced herself out of bed, her feet into her sheepskin slippers, and tied her dressing gown around her. The sheets Marigold had in her hand were, by the looks of things, mostly dry, but unmistakeably stained, a pale brown soaking a good third of the surface, with a redder brown edge where whatever liquid it was had reached. Laurel forced her mind quickly back to see if there was any way she could have done something, anything she could have knocked over, but came up blank. But as she took the sheets from Marigold she smelled the by-now familiar scents of larkspur and dried elder and felt something inside her sink. She felt nauseated.

"I don't know I..." she said helplessly. She wanted to try and explain but she had so few concrete facts and her head felt all fuzzy.

"Maybe Tibbs knocked something over," Marigold said. If it sounded like she was clutching at straws then she was. Tibbs was not a regular cat and it wasn't like him to knock things over – and in any case he still needed something to knock over, of which there was no sign – no broken vase or upended teacup nothing.

"Maybe," said Laurel, non-committal. "Do you need help sorting them?" Honestly, she just wanted to get back to sleep.

"No, I can make it work," said Marigold. "It's just that it's colour printing so I can't do it at uni and..."

"Marigold, seriously, let me. Or if you email the printer again I'll pick them up, okay."

"Okay, but then we'll need to fold and stuff them and I wanted to do that today."

"It's okay. We'll sort it. If necessary, I'll get some folks round to help. I don't know what happened but with all the tea and potions and herbs in this place... I'm sorry if it was me, Marigold, I really am."

It didn't matter that they had a plan for resolving it, and that there was no real harm done except for some extra hassle at a time they really didn't need it. But Laurel felt awful about the whole thing, and couldn't shake herself out of it. When they both got home she'd tell Marigold about the scent, about how there'd been more weird things happening with it or associated with it than Marigold was aware of, and they'd put their heads together and work everything out. They *would* be able to work everything out, so why did everything feel so awful right now?

Laurel looked at her much reduced succulent collection. At the height of her business, she had had more than three times this number, but the rate of turnover had been high as well; as soon as she'd started infusing a new batch with a particular spell she'd be packaging up a batch that was ready to go, placing them in the little cardboard boxes she'd found that worked perfectly for her purpose, adding the little labels that had been pre-printed with her care instructions on one side and on which she wrote a little handwritten message. On most it was simple – she wrote, "I hope this brings you..." and then whatever the intention of the potion was: peace, or prosperity. If she knew the customer and that they'd appreciate it, she wrote something that alluded more to magic or something a bit more spiritual. And then she had an agreement with a courier company who picked them up in batches, and everything was connected to her invoicing software. She felt she'd learned so much, and was just really getting the hang of it. It was a shame to let it go so soon, but she told herself she was on to new adventures.

Sometimes people would put in custom orders, and she'd do her best to make new potions for that. That would be on hold, as would the marketing. But Sorrel had enough magic to dilute her infusions and then bring them up to full strength so she could keep working on her classic creations.

They wouldn't do marketing or anything, and everything would be strictly limited, just a few released every week, which might even let them put the prices up. It would give Sorrel some pocket money, and maybe a bit to save for uni, cover the business overheads, and even though Laurel probably wouldn't get much income out of it, it meant that in two years, if they came back to Wellington, she could get back to it with it in good shape, and if they ended up elsewhere she could start up similar where she was and either sell the Wellington branch or hire someone to run it properly.

Her business was definitely something that she had mixed feelings about saying goodbye to. And yet at the same time, it felt like the plans she had put in place for it showed how far she'd come, and how much she might be able to do in the future.

She'd come a long way from working in cafés, and she had zero wish to go back. There was nothing wrong with making coffee, but everything was wrong with the low pay and the control over your time, and that was with the *better* employers.

Laurel found Marigold clearing everything off the dining table and then taking some pictures of it.

"What are you up to?" she asked.

"I mean, I don't think any of this furniture is worth taking with us. If you want to give some to anyone, we'll do that, and then probably we can sell the rest. I'm not doing anything without talking to you, don't worry, and not until the wedding's over. I was just kinda at a loose end. Nothing on the list I could do but too twitchy to just sit there."

"You do need to take a break sometimes," Laurel said, helping put everything back onto the table and then slouching down into an armchair. "It feels weird. Like, I know it's not *good* furniture, but I spent a long time collecting most of it, and the idea of replacing it all at once seems astronomical."

Marigold turned round with glee. "We're going to Scandinavia! All that flat-pack furniture!"

Laurel made a face. "Really?"

"Hey, you're going to scream when you realise how expensive furniture is here. Really. I can't wait – I've got my set of allen keys ready."

"I sort of hoped we'd choose things with a bit more history."

"We're probably only going to be there two years. I sort of wanted to keep it easy. Okay, how's this. I use wedding money for the basics – like a bed to start, and something to sit on – and then you can hunt through flea markets for whatever you want... and well, if there's anything we really want to keep from this lot, I'll get a quote on how much it would cost to send. Also, check with your cousins, I'm sure you have some of them flatting who might appreciate some free stuff."

"Not that coffee table, that's for sure."

In acknowledgement, the table creaked and Laurel was sure the surface became more uneven. She looked around suspiciously. It didn't seem worth taking furniture, not at the amount it cost to send it, and especially as Marigold's contract was only two years. A few favourite items would stay with Marigold's father, but other than that, all these pieces – scratty though they were, and it at least one case liberated from a skip bin – would go. They weren't worth much, definitely not the storage fees, and some nine-teen-year-old would make good use of them, but she still felt a sadness – they had been with her so much of her life.

"I'm just really good at assembling flatpack furniture," Marigold said, raising her hands. "I don't have many other skills..."

"MARIGOLD ANN NIGHTFIELD, YOU HAVE A PhD AND ARE A WITCH AND YOU CAN PLAY THE CLARINET – what more do you want?"

"Meh. It's just satisfying."

"Okay. Fine. You let me get some really old pieces from a flea market or something and I'll permit your IKEA heathenry."

"Heathenry. You speak of such from a long line of witchcraft."

"Hmm. I think it's worshipping the Norse gods that's called heathenry now. Which is appropriate being Sweden and all."

"Gods... gods have never been for me. I don't think I could do the type of witchcraft that's about worship."

"It's complicated. I mean. I don't think of gods as... yknow, people with lots of power. It's more about forces of nature. And offering to them is more about acknowledging my small place in the universe and keeping everything in balance."

Marigold laughed and started photographing the sofa, measuring it and writing down details on her laptop. Balance was not her thing and she didn't see that changing. She supposed Laurel had enough for both of them.

Laurel paused. Talking to Marigold had always been so easy and now all of a sudden she was finding it close to impossible. Eventually, she managed to blurt out even just a fraction of what had been causing her distress.

"Do you ever feel like you had really strong dreams but you can't remember any of what they are?"

"Nope, not really, mine are always really clear detail. They don't always make sense but... oh, you're saying you had really strong dreams last night..."

"Yeah. At least I think so."

"Do you know what sort? Like, were they nightmares or good dreams or..."

"I think maybe anxiety? That would make sense, what with everything going on."

"Anything I can do to take the stress off?"

"You're doing it. I think I just need to push through."

"That's entirely fair. And look, could be worse, you could be casting forgetfulness spells on yourself like I've heard my great-grandmother did in the run-up to her wedding. She was so stressed she tried to pretend it wasn't happening."

The idea seemed momentarily tempting. Then she laughed.

"Nothing that extreme. Just. Don't expect to be introducing me to anyone in Sweden because I'm sleeping for at least the first couple of months."

"OK. Except I give it two days before you're out talking to people at flea markets and plant shops and also have located at least one cousin."

"Ha! I do actually have a cousin in Sweden you know, though I've never met him. Different city though, but he knows where to get magical supplies where we are. Apparently, there's a shop just near the university."

"Right. If you end up making friends with the people running it in the first two months then you owe me cake."

"Am I that predictable?" Laurel asked.

"I like it. You have this whole web of connections and you like to pull people into it."

"I always feel like you're the confident one, the one who starts talking to strangers."

Marigold shrugged.

"I'm just... completely shameless about approaching people. I've learned some people are going to hate me on sight anyway and if I pretend to be like them then either I exhaust myself or my façade falls away dramatically and then they hate me even more. I find it easier to make sure I'm super enthusiastic about everything and then just roll with it and let them either embrace it or look like they're the weird ones. It, uh, mostly works"

"Like you turned up at my flat looking for monsters, that sort of confidence."

"Exactly that. Though it wasn't just that. I was pretty excited about getting to meet your monster and that always helped."

"And you liked meeting me."

"Of course I did. But I didn't know that until after. But I knew to ask like I was completely enthusiastic – about the monster and also about meeting you – and maybe that made it true. Or maybe as soon as I got a sight of you I realised that you were far more exciting than any monster."

Laurel cracked up. It was absolutely a compliment, but the sort of compliment only Marigold could come up with.

"I'll put that on my CV, shall I. Business cards. Laurel Windflower. More exciting than any monster..."

But when they were done talking, anxiety set in. She went back and picked up the card that had come with the herbs. She recognised the handwriting. She knew it very well.

On a still night, with the curtains open so they could see right across the harbour, to the lights on the far side, they carried on the preparations. Marigold had decided to learn to crochet and was finding it calming when it went well and a nightmare when it didn't, and she was trying to focus on that while listening to Laurel.

Laurel sat with her legs pulled up onto the sofa cushions, leaning against the corner, with her laptop balanced on top, going through the invite responses.

"Yes from Millie and Anneke," she said, as she updated her list.

Marigold jumped down from the stool where she'd been sitting swinging her legs.

"And an alpaca?"

"Just says Millie and Anneke on this."

"Well, that's a shame. We did explicitly say on the invites that alpaca don't take up the plus-one slot, right?"

"We did not."

"Pffff. I'll update the list. Who else?"

"Aw, Gran's coming!" Laurel suddenly found herself teary.

"Oh yay, I wasn't sure..."

"No, she's not young, but it would take a lot for her to miss a family wedding... hmm, I wonder if we can hire a wheelchair so she doesn't have to walk from the carpark... I'll talk to her about it. Then we have Jenna and Kez, they're uni friends of mine, you remember we met them at the Matariki fireworks last year?"

"Ah yep." Marigold entered a few things into the spreadsheet. "Turning out to be a good-sized wedding."

"Yep. I'm glad to have got past the terrified no-one will come at all stage."

"You were worried about that? With your family?"

"I mean, not really worried. Just, you feel like maybe everyone has better things to do and you're going to be there feeling embarrassed and apologising to the caterers. I just... y'know, when I was growing up and people mentioned me getting married, it just seems like the biggest lie, and even though obviously there was a reason for that it still means that right now none of it feels quite real."

"Okay, I get it, but honestly, your lot is so excited for you, you do not need to worry. Also. Look at all these couples. With or without alpaca. Your family is coming out of the closet at the rate of something, either that or we're converting them all."

"I know right. Aunt Penelope! Who would have thought?"

"Well. I'm starting to just assume people are bi unless they say otherwise. World's easier that way."

"Ha. I mean. I try not to make assumptions but it would have been easier growing up with that, that's for sure. Even if it had just been assumed that we might be."

"Mmm-hmm".

Marigold buried her head in her crochet. After a few moments Laurel gently asked, "What's wrong, Marigold?"

"Just. Wondering if my grandmother would have wanted to come to this wedding." She turned her head to one side, resting on the crochet, looking vaguely in Laurel's direction. "I think so – I mean, she was pretty supportive of me being generally weird but I don't think she specifically knew I was queer and I can't know for sure that she'd have been happy. And then I hear all these responses from your family and I'm happy they'll be there but I'm sad as well. Not because I don't want them to be there! I do! I like your family even if they get a bit noisy sometimes and don't bring the alpaca with them. I just... I just wish I had more people of my own. I have good people. I'm not that much of an extrovert. Just. A few more. Cousins. I wish..."

Her voice trailed off. Laurel looked up at her.

"I miss her sometimes..."

Laurel stood up, wrapped her arms around Marigold.

"I wish she could be here too. I would have loved to have known her."

"She'd have liked you, I think," Marigold said. "It's also because I don't have many cousins and no siblings, and my mother's coming but she's *super not into weddings*, so the imbalance just feels a bit more obvious, you know."

"Yes, I can see that. And look, not all these cousins are going to respond. It's not going to be as unbalanced as this list looks. I know for a fact one is going to be in the Himalayas but there'd be hell to pay if I didn't send an invite so away one goes."

"Yeah." Marigold wiped her eyes. "I don't mind you having more people than me. The most important ones are going to be there. Dad's pretending to be chill about it but he's seriously excited. Getting a new suit tailored and everything. And he's been really leaning into the scruffy expert look lately, so that's a big deal."

"Aw," Laurel said. Marigold's father theoretically lived in Wellington, but in practice he spent most of his time overseas. Laurel hadn't got to spend very much time with him, but he already felt like part of her family, someone who had always been there. She was glad that even if Marigold's family was small, they were supportive.

She just wished that family support was enough.

Laurel held things together as long as she could, forcing herself to joke about wedding guests, to keep herself busy working through the endless to-do lists. Every time she tried to talk to Marigold she lost courage, saying she was just anxious about her parents or her dress or something else Marigold was happy to reassure her about. It all lasted until she spilled some sugar, and then everything came out all at once, words overtaking each other.

"...and I should have told you heaps earlier – I mean I've told you a bit of it but not enough so you could tell there's a pattern – but I didn't know how to make sense of it all and I didn't know what was important and what wasn't and it hasn't so much been bad as really weird, like not magic weird more creepy weird and it just. I'm sorry. It freaked me out."

"Laurel," Marigold said, in a reversal of their usual positions. "Slow down. Start from the beginning. Please."

Laurel did her best to slow down and start from the beginning, though she was fighting back tears the whole way. She started with the whole collapse after they'd been to the fitting for her dress, and how she'd assumed it was just stress but noticed the distinct smells of burnt juniper and green willow as she came to. Still, she didn't think that much of it until the envelope was left outside, and then there was whatever had spilled on the information sheets Marigold had made, and then the posy and the door and then and then...

"And every incident I sort of found a way to dismiss and everyone was saying things were weird because I was stressed or I had a lot on my plate and I guess they were right that I was and did but the whole thing just wasn't adding up really and I didn't know what to do about it."

"You have some theories? About what's been happening?"

Laurel wrapped her arms around herself as if she were cold.

"Not good ones. I thought maybe someone wanted to stop the wedding happening, or make it a disaster, and that was why what happened was associated with the dress, and then those info sheets. But it didn't really make sense – I mean, why would people want to do that – and more to the point just about everything I'm doing at the moment is somehow related to the wedding, so if someone wanted to target me it's kinda obvious that it would end up connecting with things to do with the wedding in some way or another irrespective. And I don't... I don't know who would want to hurt me."

The last bit came out all in a rush.

Marigold frowned, looking serious.

"No. No, I don't know who would want to hurt you either."

"There's more," Laurel said, looking stricken. "I looked up the meanings of green willow and juniper and larkspur – I couldn't find much in the usual resources, one cures a headache – well, everything apparently cures a headache, nothing exciting there. So I started going through the family spell book, and I found much more stuff there. Apparently, larkspur's linked to self-deception and not seeing things as they truly are, to being misguided." Laurel looked up briefly to see if Marigold was noticeably reacting. "And there was another bit about green willow, a whole page this time, which said it was linked to reluctance or wanting to break promises so I thought about that and about how impossible it seemed that whoever had not only left things at our door and got away so quickly but somehow, despite the wards we have set up, managed to pour whatever it was on the invitation thingy, and, and, and then it didn't make sense and I don't know if I should be telling you this – oh shit, Marigold, I'm really sorry, I'm really sorry."

"Laurel. What did you do?"

"I looked again at the card that came with the posy. And the way I do loops in my Fs and Ms, quite a lot of people have commented on that, well it's the same. And then if it's about self-deception – I think I must have written it, Marigold, I think I must have written it and forgotten about it or convinced myself I didn't and what you said about the forgetfulness spells..."

Marigold looked like death.

"Laurel, what are you saying?"

"I think I must have been somehow subconsciously trying to sabotage the wedding."

"What? No, that can't be true."

"I'm really sorry... I didn't... I must have..."

"What the fuck, Laurel?" Marigold felt cold, a chill growing with every passing second.

"I still want to get married, I still want to be with you, I don't even know how it happened, I guess I was just scared or something."

"It's pretty hard to know we're making the right choice when your subconscious tried to sabotage our wedding!!! Like, do you know how that sounds?"

"Wait! I... I know exactly how it sounds I just..."

"Yeah, I'm sorry. I'm too upset to talk about it just now – I'm sorry."

"Please believe me! I love you! I want to be with you!" Laurel could hear the desperation in her own voice as she said it.

"But how can I believe it. You say you want to be with me. You say you're good with moving to Sweden, even though you love this city, even though you have a great business that you'll have to abandon, and probably when you say it you even believe it, you think it's true. How can I know that it's really true? How can I know that you won't work it out sooner or later and hate being with me, or worse I end up trapping you into a life where you're never happy and never quite sure why."

"Marigold..."

"I'm too upset to talk right now. I'm going to my dad's for the weekend. We can talk later, okay."

Laurel watched and tried to hold off crying as Marigold threw a few things into a tote bag and, without looking back, shut the door of the apartment carefully behind her, and left. It would almost have been easier if she'd slammed it, but Marigold was so reasonable she couldn't bear it.

She tried to be calm and reasonable too. Give Marigold space. She did the dishes and wiped down the kitchen bench. She put the towels in the washing machine. Then she scrolled through her phone looking for someone to call. Someone she could talk to about all this. She needed someone desperately. But who? Her best friend, Connor, who basically turned everything into a joke as a defence mechanism? Her mother, who was so focused on this wedding that it was all she could think about?

She loved them, and they were helpful to her in other circumstances – as of course she was to them – but right now, for this? When she just wanted to cry on someone? That person didn't really exist for her. Laurel had always thought herself the lucky one, with the sprawling family that mostly got on well with each other. She was realising that might be good for filling seats at weddings and for camping out on long Christmas holidays at the beach, but somehow, for things like this, she just didn't have a person.

Or more accurately, the person was Marigold.

And she couldn't bear the thought that maybe it wasn't anymore.

Laurel dried her eyes and forced herself to get on with things. Marigold had said they'd talk about things, and there wasn't anything helpful she could do between now and then. Either they'd find a way to resolve things or they wouldn't, and aside from doing anything else bad, there was little she could do to influence the outcome now. For now, she knew she had to give Marigold space – and take space herself. She just wasn't sure she could handle the loneliness that came with it.

Normally when she felt like this she knew the best thing to do was to keep herself busy, but her whole life was exploding with busyness. So she went for the second option, and did what any true Wellingtonian would do – made herself a coffee in her keep cup, pushing the lid on tight, and set up to walk up a hill.

Marigold did have a person for things like this, but it took her several hours of lying face down on the bed that had been her grandmother's, doing absolutely nothing, before she was able to sit up, make herself a large cup of tea, and message Memory.

She told people she'd been friends with Memory more years than she could count, which was an abject lie. She could remember the exact point at which they'd become friends and it was very easy to simply count forward from there and arrive at a precise answer. But at some point, the precise number had ceased to matter. Memory was there, and always had been, and felt like she'd always be, perhaps the most reliable member of her family.

Memory didn't mind Marigold just calling her, but Marigold hated to be on the receiving end of unexpected calls so much that even though she logically knew it didn't affect Memory the same way, she felt her brain screaming if she tried. So she messaged, asking if she had time for a call.

Memory replied to her almost immediately and before long Marigold was seated in the corner of the lab she still had mostly set up on the lowest floor of her father's house, hunched on a beanbag, with her laptop propped up in front of her, and Memory's face comfortingly visible on the screen.

"You had a fight with Laurel," was the first thing Memory said. "Are you okay?"

"I don't know. How did you know."

"Well, you're obviously upset. You're experiencing heaps of stress with the wedding and the move and everything else which is bound to cause some tension between the two of you. And if you were upset about some science thing, like your results being wonky or not being able to find one of those bugs you were looking for, then you'd have launched straight into it in chat."

Marigold nodded, tearfully. "I don't think it's the wedding, or the move, or the stress. I mean, it might make things worse but it's more than that. I don't think Laurel wants to get married."

"Doesn't want to get married-married or doesn't want to be with you?"

"I don't know, I don't even know if she knows."

"Okay, tell me what happened. Tell me right from the beginning."

Marigold's mind flooded with everything. Everything that could have conceivably led to this point. The day she met Laurel. The day she decided to research monsters which was what led her to meet Laurel. The day she was born! The long history of witchcraft in their families. It was totally overwhelming, and she ended up staring blankly at the screen, desperate for anyone to untangle this mess.

Memory had known Marigold for a long time.

"Okay, tell me the important things that have happened today, and I'll ask what I need to know to understand them."

Somehow, with stops and starts, Marigold was able to explain the whole thing to Memory.

"Do you think she was only trying to sabotage it because it was important to her, though?" she suggested. "Not because she didn't want it, but because she was scared of how important it was to her?"

Marigold reached under the bed and dragged out a large orange ankylosaurus toy that had been hers since she was a pre-schooler and which she kept there for emergencies. This was *definitely* an emergency. She clutched it to her chest.

"She doesn't want it because she does? Does that make it better or worse?"

"Maybe think about it being less she doesn't want it, and more than she's overwhelmed by the whole idea?"

Marigold nodded, burying her face in the Ankylosaurus. Memory was one of the few people she could be herself in front of, lean in to behaviours others thought of as childish. Like having emergency plush dinosaurs, for example. She tried to understand what Memory had just suggested. Laurel was overwhelmed? Marigold understood overwhelmed, but she didn't orchestrate sabotage she didn't remember, she mostly just stopped functioning when things got too much.

"If Laurel is overwhelmed I want to help her."

"For sure, and that instinct is one of the reasons you're a good friend to me. But maybe she needs some quiet and some space to process it."

"I don't mind giving her quiet. I can do that. But if this whole thing happens every time she gets overwhelmed – I can't deal with the whodunnits and the secrecy and the not knowing."

"That's fair. But I think you may be getting a bit ahead of yourself. This is something that's happened, it's not necessarily a course ahead for the future."

Marigold nodded. Everything was far too much. When she'd talked it through with Memory she went and found some old facial scrub she'd left in a cupboard and scrubbed the dirty tears from her face until her skin was raw and smelled of toothpaste. It oddly felt a bit better. If Laurel had told her she was having second thoughts, told her she might have misjudged, she'd have been upset, of course, but she could have talked to her about it. The idea that she might have hidden it so deeply she didn't even know she had those concerns herself, well that was something else entirely, and it terrified Marigold. She didn't know how she could ever be safe, how she could ever trust her when all along, deep down, she didn't want to be with her at all.

But for now, she tried to follow Memory's guidance. Take a break. Take it a bit at a time. She grabbed her gardening gloves and secateurs and headed out into the garden.

About an hour later, her face red and smarting in the wind, Laurel made it up to the top of the hill where what had for some years been Wellington's sole wind turbine. Even though they'd since added a whole group of them at Makara it was still the only one – a test of the prototype, getting people used to the idea – visible from much of the city. Laurel had been up here before, probably in her first year in the city, but it had been a long time. The track was narrow, running along the outside of the long predator-proof fence that enclosed the wildlife sanctuary.

From here, you could see across much of the city laid out, the whole harbour blue, with the adjoining Hutt City on the other side and then following its way up a river valley until it was out of view. She could see past the cranes on the waterfront, the airport off to the side on a rare piece of flat land that had once been submerged, making the hill of the Miramar peninsula next to it an island. A ferry was heading in at the entrance, past the lighthouse on the other side, and a few little boats left trails of white across the harbour. Most of the suburbs, white on green, the painted weatherboard houses in among the green, and the purplish tones the hills began to take on as dusk crept closer.

She *did* love this city. If everything else in her life was falling desperately to pieces, then at least she would still have it, at least she would still be welcome here.

She turned around, spinning herself beneath the huge blades.

Wellington, though small on a global scale, was always bigger than you could see, hiding behind its hills and its greenbelt; even up somewhere high like this, with its panoramic views, little bits of it were trapped from view, clustering in valleys like creases on a crumpled table cloth. Some parts of the city, it was said, were designed in London by men with wigs who had never seen its hills, and that was why some roads turned to flights of stairs, and others stopped abruptly, continuing on a nearby hill. The land punctured any design imposed upon it, and she liked that.

Laurel had been pushing the details of what happened away from her head, unable to handle thinking about it too much, but now she let them sink in. None of it really made sense. Had she really been subconsciously sabotaging her wedding, her relationship? The person she loved and what she most wanted for her life. It had made so much sense in the moment, to the point she had been prepared to admit to it, even though she had no memory and no motive beyond the old lack of confidence rearing its head. What she'd been all too ready to admit to, horrified by herself, now seemed too much by the light of day. She looked around. She didn't have the ingredients for the spells she wanted to carry out, nor were there easily available alternatives. But she did find a smooth piece of amethyst and she had the plants that had been left outside their door in her pocket. It was enough. She circled the herbs three times with the amethyst, and then she held the herbs together and circled all of them over her head three times, breathing deeply and holding her focus as she did so. Then she spoke out loud:

Show me now and show me true,

Show me the garden where you first grew.

Rhyming was not necessary for spells – before widespread literacy, it was probably to help people remember them. But Laurel was so used to spells rhyming that it was comforting, in a way, putting her in her right mind.

She held out the stick of grass in her hands. Nothing happened for a few moments, and then it glowed, flew up in the air and then out over the city. It should have been too small to see, as it whirled and blew far away, but she kept track of it, focusing with her eyes, until it came to a halt, glowing and suspended in air, glowed brighter for a few minutes and then grew longer, an impossibly tall beam of light that seemed to stretch as long as the ground and then up into the sky, beyond anything Laurel could see. Then, just as quickly, it disappeared into nothingness, leaving nothing behind but the regular light of the day, and it didn't really seem like it had ever been there at all.

Laurel stared and watched, fixing the location firmly in her mind. It wasn't anywhere she was ever likely to have gone looking for herbs. She checked Google Maps, which revealed there to be a garden centre almost exactly in that location. She certainly didn't know anyone who lived there, so it was the obvious explanation. And it would never have even occurred to Laurel to get herbs from a garden centre. If it was too rare for her or someone she knew to be able to give her a cutting of, it was definitely too rare to just come across in a garden centre.

So maybe this wasn't her doing after all. At least not all of it. Perhaps the fainting outside of the dress shop could have been all in her head, but the package through the door and the spilled potion, they were someone else's doing. Maybe a small part of her had been to try and sabotage her wedding, but most of it wasn't, and there was definitely someone else at work here.

Laurel sat down on the grass, on what felt like the top of the world, and tried to decide what to do next.

Marigold pulled on her gardening gloves and began to tackle the herb garden. It was not too hard to keep a handle on, as long as she kept up to it – it was neat and well-tended, mostly short plants rather than anything too bushy or out of hand, and the little paths running between the beds made it easy to take care of. Marigold's grandmother had put a lot of thought into how it was set up, and there was definitely some magical protection going on too.

Still, witches valued work even more than they valued magic, and even if said grandmother could have made a garden that didn't need tending she wouldn't have done. It was part of witchcraft to be close to your supplies – oh it was okay to buy them, if you had to, but you still had to spend time getting to know them. And so Marigold kneeled on a little cushion and clipped back a dying leaf here and pulled out a stray bit of grass or some other weed there. It was almost meditative, and made her feel a little better about the situation, or at least stopped her from feeling her full feelings which was what she needed.

As she gardened she noticed the different level of connection she had to the plants now. She had always loved tending this garden – she liked plants, it connected her to her witch ancestors, and more specifically it felt like the last thing she could do for her grandmother. She hadn't realised just how very different it would be to be doing this when actually a witch. Connections she couldn't describe even now, and certainly wouldn't have been able even to attempt before she experienced them for herself.

And soon she was going to lose it all.

No. She forced herself to stop thinking about that. Ruminating was the last thing she needed to be doing. Marigold was still a witch. She still had magic. Magic couldn't solve everything – if only – but it could give her the edge. She had an advantage, access to something few other people did.

She wanted things to be like they had been only a couple of days ago. She wanted things to be right. She wanted to be *happy*.

She was less experienced than other witches her age, of course, but the other research she'd done on magic and associated matters had given her something of the edge. She started working through the possibilities she was aware of. She knew *love spells* were immoral, not that they really worked as they seemed to in books. Manipulating people into doing something was acceptable only in extreme circumstances, but to manipulate them into thinking or feeling a certain way was taboo, and for good reason.

There was magic to work with her own feelings, of course. She could calm herself down, she could prioritise one thing over another, she could work out what she really wanted. Except she knew what she wanted, she was just unsure if she could have it. She didn't *want* this to end, but she also didn't want to stay if it was all a lie, if Laurel didn't want to be part of it even if she thought she did. She would rather have nothing than something fake, something where Laurel was secretly miserable below the surface.

She pulled her hoodie up over her head and down onto her face and told herself that even though the timing seemed terrible it made sense because she could go off to

Sweden alone and unencumbered and be an entirely new person. She told herself that really hard and yet she couldn't make herself believe it.

Then she took cuttings, rosemary and sage. She burned a small piece of wood until it was black, and collected some rainwater from the tank.

She boiled the rainwater, added the herbs and the blackened wood, making a potion. She soaked linen in it and, because it was late outside, she hung it in the bathroom and switched the extractor fan on. This was a spell to give her clarity, and when it dried her answer would be on the cloth. Except she didn't need to wait for it to dry to know what the answer would be.

She wanted to be with Laurel.

Laurel wanted to be with her.

So what in the world was going on?

Laurel's first urge was to run to Marigold to tell her that it was all solved, that it was going to be okay again. But something was stopping her. It felt like it would just be heaping more frantic emotion on the fire. She needed to give her space. She needed to work out what the hell was happening.

Even though there seemed to be someone out there sabotaging them, it was actually a relief to know that it – at least mostly – hadn't been her. It gave her some hope that things could be fixed, even though it seemed so difficult right now.

Still, it was a miserable evening in the apartment, not knowing if they'd ever have the life back they shared, ever have their little routines, if she'd ever get to hear Marigold crashing around in the kitchen as she baked again. She didn't have a meal. She snacked on pretzels and ate tuna right from the can. She forced herself to try and sleep, alone, with every little noise outside being amplified; every car that drove past, every drip of water, every rumble that might be an earthquake but was probably just the washing machine upstairs. When she finally got up, even the simplest of tasks – cleaning her teeth, pouring her cereal – made her feel like she was moving through thick, thick sludge. Only the fact that she had made progress, that she knew something of what had been happening, the fact that the relationship and the rest of the plans she'd been carefully making for the rest of her life might be salvageable, kept her feeling like it might be worth it after all.

But even if she could convince herself – convince herself and Marigold – that they weren't responsible, the answer wasn't looking like it was going to be a happy one. It was very hard not to come to the conclusion that someone was trying to sabotage their wedding. Which of course raised a whole heap more questions than it answered, not just about who but also about how and what on earth their motivations might be. If it really was someone who was distressed at not being invited, that meant someone Laurel or Marigold was close to – or at least someone who thought they were close – was showing some serious red flags.

She hated the idea that there was someone like that, and, worse, not knowing who it was meant that it could be anyone. She felt like she couldn't trust anyone. But slowly the pieces started to go together. She could see parts of what had happened and eventually they started to fit into something coherent enough to try and explain to Marigold.

"It's another fucking spell gone wrong."

"Sorrel?" Marigold asked. The previous summer Laurel's young cousin Sorrel had gotten into a scrape by trying to cast a memory spell to get them through their exams. Spells gone wrong were practically a coming-of-age ritual for young witches. Sorrel wasn't the first and wouldn't be the last.

"Not this time, I think they've learned their lesson. And I'm not sure it was quite that innocent either."

"Tell me," Marigold said.

Laurel reminded Marigold about how she had discovered what kind of witch she was. A storage witch, they jokingly called it, because it made them think of convenient plastic drawers from the Warehouse, which... well there was no inherent reason plastic couldn't be involved in witchcraft, but most established spells, not to mention the whole witchy aesthetic, were based around an old fashioned look and the use of natural materials. That she and Marigold both had taken on the abilities of long-dead witches, and that Laurel's discovery explained how good she was at growing succulents, had given her the idea of infusing them with particular properties.

That, she felt, was at the heart of where the answer to what had been happening would be found.

Carefully, sitting down together, they made a list of the possible culprits – people who might wish them harm, or who at least would be willing to sacrifice their wedding, and in an underhand way no less, in service of some bigger and more important cause. It seemed an easy enough exercise on the face of it. The trouble was, there wasn't much of a list. Neither of them had exes who hadn't thoroughly moved on. Their families were both in support of the whole thing – even if they had opinions about some of the specifics, it was the event of the year in both families and none of them could want it to not go ahead. The odd younger member of the family might find it something that was boring to be dragged to, but that hardly raised them to the level of sabotage.

This was a new one for them. And neither of them felt like they had many enemies. Competitors, possibly, people they annoyed, for sure. But this seemed to be more personal than that. Laurel considered and then rejected that it was someone in the extended family who objected to it being a same-sex marriage. Witches were not exactly known for their conservatism.

They paused, both thinking uncomfortable thoughts, not quite looking at each other.

"Is it possible they have some reason they don't want us to get married but don't have anything against us personally?" Marigold asked.

Laurel shrugged. "Anything's possible. Like what though?"

"Time travellers." Marigold said, rather too definitively, before sipping at her hot blackcurrant. "If our marriage triggers something that has a later impact on the world –

like someone isn't where they need to be when something else happens because they're at our wedding, some sort of interdimensional rift, yadda yadda yadda."

"Okay. So I know magic's real, but time travel, even for a witch, feels like a step too far."

"Oh, I agree. Just brainstorming ideas here."

"Okay, does anyone hate one of us? Does anyone *like* one of us and think she should be marrying them instead?"

Marigold shook her head. "I really don't think any of my exes have thought about me in a long time."

"Mine neither. And I haven't *noticed* anyone appearing to have a crush on either of us, have you?"

Everything they came up with seemed to come to a dead end. After all the puzzles they'd unpicked and solved together, this one, which seemed to be centred directly around them, was the one that seemed impossible for them to find the answer to.

"This is all so weird and dramatic. Ugh! I know we get dramas sometimes but they're like, monsters are unhappy with us over a misunderstanding, or ancient evil awakening... not even ancient evil, just ancient vaguely grumpy dude with magic. This is about *people* and their *relationships* and *feelings* and it's super gross."

"And weird bad timing as well... hang on, is it possible it's more about stopping us going to Sweden more than stopping us getting married. I mean, I know we don't need to be married, but it's part of the whole plan."

"What could we possibly get up to in Sweden."

"Maybe it's something we need to do here. Something we need to be around for. They're quite possibly not trying to hurt us at all, maybe our feelings don't even factor into it because it's something much bigger and more important than us."

Laurel stretched herself out and made a displeased face. "It just feels shit. Like. You're right, it may not be malicious and it may not be anyone we care about, but I had to fight so hard to be okay with the idea of myself being queer, and even then I didn't picture myself as the sort of person who could get married, it just wasn't on the table. I feel like I deserve for it to be easy, you know? It sounds very entitled but..."

"No, it's not. You do deserve better. I just wish I could make it happen for you."

"Well, I wouldn't want anyone else." Laurel forced a grin despite everything and Marigold returned it.

"No. Nor would I."

"Laurel," Marigold almost screamed, spinning round from the windowsill to where Laurel was sitting at the dining table with her laptop. "It's your succulents."

Laurel looked up. "What."

"Clara. My ancestor Clara Oleander."

Laurel started to shake. "Slow down, please."

"Oh fuck, this is all my fault. I'm so sorry and I thought it was you I let you think it was you."

"Marigold," Laurel said, getting up and guiding her to a seat. "Please explain to me what is going on. Short words. Like I'm a child."

Marigold was gasping for words, as if she was about to start sobbing.

"Remember Clara," she said.

"Of course. I basically have half her brain inside me."

"Dubious and inaccurate description, but I know what you mean," Marigold replied. There was nothing like saying something inaccurate or imprecise to snap Marigold out of a panic. Laurel had, in fact, taken on the magical ability of Clara Oleander, one of Marigold's ancestors, back when they first met, back when she was still working out what kind of a witch she was.

"You were right, it was a spell gone wrong. It was my spell."

"What was the spell."

"Uh, so I was really stressed about the wedding. And everyone in my family likes you, but you know the whole neurodivergence runs in families thing? Except I'm bouncy neurodivergent but most of them are flat affect, monosyllabic, hyper-introverted neurodivergent, you know."

"And that's fine. You know that's fine, it always has been."

"Yes, but I was scared your family wouldn't get it and think they didn't like them or were being standoffish or something. So I tried making a spell so that they would understand each other. And I thought a lot about how people just see us as brains and having logical thought, and don't understand we have feelings too, just because we don't show it in the obvious ways."

"That uh, sounds like a complicated spell, especially for a new witch."

"I thought it was just a getting-along spell."

"But it doesn't tell me what this has to do with Clara or succulents."

"Okay, so whatever remains of Clara, who up to now hasn't really been a person or someone with emotions, I mean not since she died. She really is just knowledge and intellect, not just someone stereotyped as such. Suddenly she starts having feelings and wanting to get along with people, except the people she's most connected to you, other than you, are your succulents."

"This whole thing sounds weird. I'm fond of my succulents but I'm not sure they're... people."

"Yes, but when you infuse them it involves Clara's magic. She gets attached to things. Remember she's not a full person, just sort of a half-ghost. And you're abandoning the succulents, so the obvious way to make things right, to her, is to stop you."

"But the note..."

"The one that said 'family'? The one in your handwriting? She got it from our notice board. It was one of the headings in an earlier version when we were working out how to invite. It must have fallen down somewhere. I worked it out when I was holding it up to the light for clues and saw the pinhole in it. Clara wants to know the succulents will be safe, that they'll be looked after."

Laurel looked at Marigold blinking for a few moments and then she grabbed her phone and made a call.

Laurel turned to Marigold and adopted her aunt's voice. "Sorrel is still young and has school, and it's a very long journey to be making alone, and who knows what might happen to them on the way down – what if they don't know when to get back on the bus after a break?"

"But we can't..." Marigold wailed, looking at their To Do list. Tauranga was an eight-hour drive each way, at least. Also, the chances of something happening to them as they tried to leave the city seemed high.

"I know," said Laurel. "I know. I'm calling Gran now."

Half an hour later and Sorrel had a ticket booked on the Intercity Bus from Tauranga down to Wellington for the next day, a safety charm made specially by Gran – who probably privately thought it was a bit over the top, but if it smoothed people's anxieties so be it, and a list of phone numbers of cousins living vaguely close to the route, including Millie and Anneke near Palmy, who would in an emergency drive out to retrieve them. Marigold had also responded to three separate texts from Laurel's family members to promise to be there at the railway station well in advance of the bus's timetabled arrival time, even though it had literally never been early ever.

Sometimes having a family matriarch was annoying. Other times it was extremely useful.

The following evening, Marigold and Laurel both met Sorrel at the railway station.

"Oh no! Do you have a coat?" Marigold proclaimed, rushing forward at the sight of Sorrel in a pink tank top above their jeans. They'd been growing their hair and their nails were painted to match the top. They had a couple of charms round their neck, one presumably Gran's for safety. Laurel cracked up at Marigold's concern while Sorrel chucked their backpack at her.

"I have one right here, *aunties*," they proclaimed, rolling their eyes as they pulled on the navy blue, slightly too-small puffer jacket. "Emergency rescue witch at your service."

Laurel hugged her cousin. "Is that your only bag?"

"Yep. You don't expect me to stay too long, do you? Mum has opinions about me having schoolwork. Apparently, she wants me to succeed like Marigold."

Laurel tried not to let that sting. Marigold's achievements were impressive, after all, but still!

"Nah, hopefully this will be quick and we'll have you on your way."

"Perhaps I can fly back."

"Ha, we'll see. Not at the amount the flights were going for today, I'm afraid."

Marigold had already ordered a rideshare and the three of them scrambled in for the short ride up to Brooklyn. Laurel felt a sudden burst of energy, like she was raring to go for the ritual, but it wouldn't be wise to count on it and more importantly it wouldn't be fair on Sorrel after spending the whole day travelling. Instead, Laurel declared it a 'pizza night' and Marigold a 'corrupt the youth with old queer movies night', telling an unimpressed Sorrel about how there was like one movie with a gay character in all year and you had to go to the special film festival to see it.

"No. Even you're not that old. That's like Aunt Millie's era. Maybe even older."

"Thanks, kid. I've sent you some links, let me know what you think."

Sorrel started scrolling on their phone.

"Wow, you really did mean old. Look at this. DEBS. But I'm a Cheerleader. Wow."

"Okay, that's enough. What would you like to recommend."

Sorrel got a wicked glint in their eye. "Do you watch anime?"

"I like Studio Ghibli," Marigold suggested.

"Okay, right, no. Okay, so deal, I watch one of your classic silent films, and you watch a couple of episodes of Yuri on Ice."

"Sounds like a plan," Marigold said. That evening, even though they knew that everything depended on the next day, and it would change everything, felt surprisingly calm. They huddled on the sofa, sharing the pizza, and for the first time in a while, both Laurel and Marigold felt okay. They wanted to capture and hold that evening forever.

"We're going to need more space for the ritual than we have here," Laurel said. Sorrel was in the shower, having apparently been quite happy with the sofa and heap of blankets. Laurel was tugging a brush through her hair, having already mainlined most of a plunger full of coffee.

"I thought we'd just go down to Central Park, find a corner somewhere. There's nowhere perfect, we just need a bit of space. Unless you'd rather head out to the beach."

"In this wind. Ideally not? But the park's pretty busy, are we going to attract attention. I don't mind if people know, but I don't want us to be interrupted."

Marigold shook her head.

"Nah, I've thought of that. There's not going to be any-where totally private, of course, but I'll put some sort of glamour on so people mind their own business and don't think we're doing anything weird. Not that weird is exactly unusual but it's good to be careful."

"I'm thinking if I bring a range of succulents, that will be sufficient. They're clearly connected via this... is it a ghost we're calling it?"

"For want of a better term. Yeah. Just choose a range of ages and types."

While Laurel put the succulents into a shallow box Marigold checked and rechecked her bag. They'd spent part of yesterday working on the spell, but they knew there were a lot of unknowns. They were dealing with both how things went for Sorrel, and the lingering part – the ghost, if you like – of a long-dead witch, temperament unknown. So Marigold was bringing plenty of extra supplies, just in case they had to do something a little different to what they had planned.

Sorrel was precise about getting dressed, in the way many teenagers are, but eventually all of them were ready. Car-rying their supplies, they made it out of the apartment and down to the hilly park, where they found themselves a corner of lawn by the bush, away from the main pathways, away from the popular playground with its flying foxes. They placed their right hands together and Marigold made a glamouring spell – it didn't make them invisible, but it did make them hard to notice, people looking past them without really registering they were there, certainly quelling their curiosity.

And then they were able to begin.

They stood in a circle around the succulents, with Marigold throwing copper salt around them. The succulents started to glow, just slightly.

"What are your powers?" she asked of them, desperately suppressing a giggle at the idea she was talking to plants. They all heard a little of it. Heard maybe wasn't the right word – because Marigold wasn't quite sure which sense she was using to detect the powers but she sensed them all the same: prosperity, love, clarity, relaxation, and she can tell the others were too.

They pushed harder together. What was within them? What was caught within them? The image that emerged was like in smoke, at least one person, then several, then one again. Then a figure stepped out of Laurel and became one with the apparition.

Laurel stepped forward.

"Clara Oleander."

The form spun around.

"Clara Oleander. This is Sorrel. They are my cousin, of the Windflower family, a young witch, a good person. They will be ensuring things are kept in my stead when I am in the far countries from here."

The witch, the ghost, the person, whatever she was, spun round, and then leaned over as if she was listening.

"I have been blessed with your powers and know it is an honour. But everything changes and I am doing my best to make sure the most important things continue."

Marigold chimed in.

"You will be safe with Sorrel and the decisions they make. And if they change things you will not scare them like you have scared us."

Marigold could have sworn she heard the plants grumble. But then the light suspended in the air wooshed into Sorrel all of a sudden, and Sorrel was grinning. Marigold took that as a good sign. Heaven knew, they looked like they were happy with the idea in any case.

"I need to stay here and sort something out," Marigold said as they packed up their stuff. "I'll be home soon."

Laurel looked concerned. "Are you sure? Will you be safe?"

Marigold forced a smile. "Yeah of course. Please. I just need a few moments. I'll explain later."

Marigold watched as Sorrel and Laurel headed uphill, their hands full of stuff, laughing and chatting, mentioning something about ice cream from the dairy on the way back. When they were quite gone – out of sight and out of earshot – Marigold took a deep breath and sat down on the grass. With any luck, what had been haunting Laurel had been dealt with and so had the threat to their wedding. While the whole thing sounded ridiculous, it was of course a major relief to know that it hadn't been Laurel subconsciously sabotaging their relationship and thus their upcoming marriage, but her plant business, of all things. Marigold did feel a bit guilty for having ever believed in the first place that it might have been her at fault, but Laurel herself had presented it to her that way so of course that was the obvious way to think. And now it was all over, and everything could come back together – they were getting married, they were moving to Sweden, they were getting whole new, exciting lives together, the sort of fairy tale ending that rarely happens in reality. They had come through this together, and they would get through things again, and they would always be all the stronger for it.

Laurel would need to work on stronger containment of any powers she had inside her, but she knew Laurel knew that more than well enough, and Marigold would be there to support her with it. That wasn't a project for today though. They had plans ahead.

Except Marigold was realising there was one thing she couldn't take with her.

That ritual had strained her, an order of magnitude more than it had affected the other two, even though she'd done her very best to hide it. But it was about more than just being magically exhausted. Being a witch took effort, for sure, but having another witch's powers was a constant conflict, one that took a lot of attention. One that came with risk.

Even Marigold Nightfield, much as she was loathe to admit it sometimes, couldn't do everything. And this needed to be her choice. She would never manage to keep her magic forever, but she could choose when to let it go, on her terms. She could choose to focus on everything else in her life: on science, on travel, on Laurel.

It would once have seemed like a difficult choice but now, even though it came at a loss, it was obvious to her that it was the right one.

She felt something above her, looked up and couldn't quite see what it was, except she knew it was a choice she had to take, a path she had to walk without grandparents, without lines of witches, without magic, but with herself, with Laurel, with the people she made her own relationships with.

Marigold reached up, not just for the immediate future, not just for the wedding, but for the whole life that lay ahead of her, for herself, for Laurel, for love.

Suddenly everything got very loud. She could see a bright light ahead of her. Then everything seemed to shatter into pieces of every different colour imaginable. What had been a vague pale purple now became a shattered spectrum of luminescent colours: reds and blues, oranges and greens, all of them cascading one after another into each other. And then they began tricking away, a cascade, a waterfall even and then it was as if Marigold was closer, close enough to see different reflections of herself or part of her life reflected in each shard, and she saw herself, the day she became a witch, and she saw one of the very first times she used that magic, making a bud on a cherry tree grow instantly to blossom.

The last of Marigold's magic dissipated. She could feel it leaving her body, as if something was deflating, but all anyone else would have been able to see was a woman looking a bit lost and a bit sad. Marigold, though, felt like something was running out of her veins, faster than she could ever hope to stop. She hadn't imagined it would happen like this, but she'd never been sure how or when it would happen so she supposed this was as likely as anything.

She should be fine now. She should be just how she was all the time before, as normal as Marigold Ann Nightfield was ever likely to get. Disappointed, perhaps, but she should be fine. She kept telling herself but it was like she could barely even hear her own internal voice anymore, and everything was a little distorted, slightly out of kilter, and yes, this was something that was inevitably going to happen and maybe this was something that needed to happen, and there was a good chance even that it was for the best that it had happened, but at that very instant, knowing any or all of that didn't make things any easier for Marigold, who was standing a bit stunned and a bit bereft, and looking vaguely out without seeing across to the playground and the two children going past one after the other on the twin flying foxes.

She didn't remember, later, walking around and up the hills, could only tell she had when she checked the fitness app on her phone. She supposed she knew this city well enough that it came naturally, that she didn't need to worry about finding her way, didn't need to think about putting one foot after another in front of each other. Whether by habit or by subconscious determinations, she made it through. She knocked on the door of their apartment even though she had a key and when Laurel opened it they sort of fell into each other's arms.

"I lost my magic," Marigold said, and she kept saying it over and over until Laurel half-guided, half-carried her inside, sat her in the comfy armchair, and put a mug of hot chocolate in her hand.

Laurel woke to find herself in bed alone. She got up and found the door open, Marigold on the steps outside that ran down the outside of the little block of apartments. Sorrel was sound asleep on the sofa, curled up with a nest of blankets as if they were more a wild animal in its nest than a teen crashing on a relative's sofa. It was still semi-dark, and there was a mist down over the suburb, a cold bite to the air. Laurel fastened her dressing gown tighter and sat down next to her.

"Missing your magic," she asked.

In response, Marigold moved her fingers, the way she would cast a light, one of the simplest spells of all. Everything stayed dark. She smiled sadly and looked down.

"I'm so sorry," Laurel said, knowing there weren't good words for a loss like this.

"I think it's for the best. I don't want to have to try and be everything at once, and there was so much pressure, to make the most of it. I ended up spreading myself too thin and I have the sort of brain that does better when it's specialised."

"I'm glad," Laurel said. "I think I'd be devastated if I lost mine."

"I'm a bit upset, to be honest. Hence the whole mopey sitting outside and having feelings before dawn thing. But I'm going to be doing a postdoc, in a country where I don't speak the main language, and that's a lot. I want to go exploring with you and eat meatballs and sit outside at cafes and hang out in warm saunas in freezing weather. I want us to hang out looking at new plants and reading books and just sitting in parks watching people go past."

"Yeah, and we're going to pretend to be Vikings. Quietly though. Do you think there were Viking witches?"

Marigold munched on her croissant.

"Viking was actually an activity rather than a civilisation. Going Viking was like going out in boats and conducting raids, and even the people who do that didn't do it all the time. They were mostly farmers and shit. In their civilisation, I'm sure they had all the normal things: weavers, blacksmiths, witches."

Laurel held out the paper bag of croissants to her.

"Sorted then. Another?"

"Yep. Because if I'm eating my feelings I'm going to do it properly, goddamn it."

As Laurel had predicted, the day of their wedding was fine. Not abnormally beautiful, the sort that would only come from magic, but blue skies with trails of white and a gentle breeze. Coming from a whole family of witches has its tensions, the weird pranks and the fact your mother *really does* always know when you're lying, but when you need a fine day for an outdoor wedding, there's absolutely no question that they'll make it happen for you.

The marriage license had space for an alternate venue, and they'd put Marigold's father's house just because it seemed superstitious not to, but in Laurel's mind at least there had never been the slightest doubt that it would go ahead here, on this lawn, surrounded by native bush, with the hills around and a clear blue sky overhead. For now, she was enjoying a few moments' peace – the calm before the storm, she joked in her head – a little silence and it felt like the whole world had melted away.

They were gathering only metres away, but she'd cast a quick spell that gave her a sort of bubble, just for a little while, dulled everything that wasn't close to her. Otherwise, it would have been unbearable. The spell had actually been one of Marigold's favourites, and it felt a little wrong to have borrowed it from her when she could no longer use it herself, but only a little. If there was anyone who had the strategies to keep herself safe and comfortable, with or without magic being involved, it was Marigold.

Outside of her bubble, she knew her parents and siblings would be there, and a large chunk of her extended family as well, along with old friends and new. She'd seen the setup, the little white chairs on the lawn, with lavender-coloured ribbons strung between them. They'd set everything they could in motion. Now all they had to do was play their part.

Marigold sat on a wooden bench just off a little trail and did her very best not to scuff her brand new shoes, instead swinging her lower legs backways and trying not to think about what was about to happen, nor about all the people who were gathering on the little lawn just uphill from them. Memory had rushed off to get something and then was back, calming her down, telling her silly jokes, anything to make the time pass faster. It was her to arrive first, and give the guests a chance to see each of them individually, but everyone had to be at their seats first, and honestly, the time couldn't come quickly enough.

Memory was looking amazing in a classic purple brides-maid's dress that had been made for her. Her thick hair, normally worn in a plait, was loose and it suited her. There was a bouquet of ferns and lavender on the bench beside Marigold, waiting for Memory to hold.

"Thank goodness I don't need to hold your train," Memory said, half-laughing at the very idea. Marigold rolled her eyes.

"Call me a stereotype, but the only train I'm thinking about is the one that crosses the bridge from Malmö to Copenhagen. We can go to Copenhagen! For a day trip. You know they've got... it's like an old theme park, but right in the centre of the city."

"You're a stereotype," Memory said. "But I love your dress."

Marigold stood up and spun round on the path, her new purple docs pinching her feet even though she'd stomped up and down the apartment stairs with her feet inside them taped every day for the past fortnight. Such was the price one pays. She twirled and the skirt of her dress spun out.

"Thank you," she said. "So do I."

"I'm going to miss you. I know we don't get to see each other that often, but it's still nice knowing you're only a few hour's drive away."

Marigold felt suddenly on the verge of tears. "Oh, oh you as well. But two years isn't long, and there's a good chance we'll come back for a visit in that time anyway. And look I know it's hard, with a baby and all that, but if you did find a way to visit please do."

Someone must have signalled Memory – Marigold had not been told about the details of this, probably because she'd invent a new code of some sort for it, which was infuriating. And then before she knew it, Marigold Ann Nightfield was walking forward, just as they'd practised. Round the corner, and she paused and took in a breath – everything was set up how they'd planned, except she hadn't quite appreciated how it would look until she got there. The white chairs with purple ribbons. The arch...

First one, then a few more, then everyone stood and turned and they were all smiling at her, so warm.

Her whole worry that there would be all Laurel's people and so few of hers seemed ludicrous now. She had her father there, waiting for her, and she had Memory right behind her, and a couple of cousins and friends from her research but so many of the people were both their people. Friends they'd made during their time together – Aishah and Tay were there, with Adam all dressed up in a tiny suit with a bowtie. Even before Jasmina had got together with Penelope they had both helped her out together, and there was Larch, her nephew and ward, possibly the first time she'd seen him out of a hoodie; he scrubbed up well and was dressed in a long-sleeved shirt. There were Mildred and Anneke, the former in an amazing woven shawl, but sadly no actual alpaca. She supposed the council *would* have had something to say about that.

But even Laurel's family, she'd spent so much time with them, they were becoming their own, were they not? Certainly, she was so pleased to see them there.

The celebrant stood beneath an arch of twisted fern fronds and lavender. Marigold made her way there, stood where she had planned, and Memory stood right there beside her. It felt like exactly where she was meant to be.

Laurel stood waiting in a little clearing of green, surrounded by native grass and ferns unfurling upward. Sorrel had grown their hair out and it was just long enough to wear up, braided and looped until it looked almost like a flower. They wore a waistcoat in the same purple as Connor's tie and Memory's bridesmaid's dress – she was yet to see the dress so far, but she was sure it was lovely, and glad Memory had been able to travel to support Marigold. She was well aware that for both of them this would be the last chance to catch up with many people who were important to their lives before they headed overseas.

The sky was blue, punctuated by fast-moving clouds. The wind started to pick up and then dulled, suddenly, to a gentle breeze. Laurel smiled. That was her family making things work for her. And it was going to be perfect. Somehow all the anxiety seemed to evaporate now it was actually happening. Nothing could change things now.

And yet there was anxiety creeping up with every minute. It wasn't about the marriage – just about being on show, on having everyone look at her. She wasn't used to that. But this was her moment and she was going to make the most of it. She looked down at her dress, glad she'd chosen something it was possible to walk in. Her blue hair – shoulder length, these days – had been twisted and pinned in a fantastically complex arrangement that she sort of loved, and didn't expect she'd ever experience again.

And then Connor had her by the shoulders and was gently moving her into place on the pathway and giving her the signal to move forward and somehow even though she had no idea what she was meant to be doing and the whole rehearsal had completely disappeared from her brain, her feet somehow knew what to do and they moved her forward, one small step after another.

She saw them all now, everyone turning to look at her, all dressed up, standing in a wave to watch her, and she walked forward, and she could see everyone there, almost everyone she loved here today – and not even casting prank spells on each other for once, just holding up the nice weather. She saw in front of them, the arch and the celebrant, and there was Memory in her purple dress that matched what Sorrel and Connor just behind her were wearing. She took a look back over her shoulder, just briefly, and smiled at them, but both of them were grinning anyway, and Connor nodded her forward.

And there at the front of all this, shifting from one foot to another barely able to hold her excitement, was Marigold. She wore a mostly white dress, but rather than a wedding dress it was her usual style, with a big skirt just below the knee, and edging around it were little purple... wait, were those dinosaurs? Had Marigold Nightfield turned up to her own wedding in a dinosaur dress. Laurel felt her heart take a leap and she wanted to laugh and cry all at once. She didn't feel like it could be possible to love Marigold more.

A bouquet of lavender in her hands, Laurel Windflower stepped forward.

A note from Andi R. Christopher

Thanks for reading! I hope you enjoyed *Weddings and Witchcraft*, the fifth and *final* book in the Windflower series. If you did, please do consider reviewing it on the site you bought it from, or on a book review site like The Story Graph or Goodreads. Every review helps.

A finished series, wow! Thank you for all your support in making it this far. My next series begins with *Tides of Magic*. It's got a lot of the things readers have told me they love in this series – magic, a New Zealand setting, queer and neurodivergent characters – but the books are a bit longer and more complex. I hope you'll find them heaps of fun – I'm really enjoying writing them.

Want more witchy fiction? Head to https://witchyficti on.com for the full list.

Huge thanks to Jamie, Jackie, Kim, Kerry, and the rest of the Witchy Fiction crew for helping me get this novella – and this whole series - out into the world. And lastly, I'd love to keep in touch with you via my newsletter. You can subscribe at https://andi.digitalpress.blog/.

About the author

Andi R. Christopher is a writer of queer urban and contemporary fantasy. Their Charley Deacon series – stories of sea magic and self discovery – begins with "Tides of Magic", out now, and their previous Windflower series comprises cosy novellas about queer witches in Aotearoa New Zealand. They also write speculative fiction as Andi C. Buchanan. You can find them online at andirchristopher.com or https://linktr.ee/andiwrites.

Also by Andi R. Christopher

Windflower Series

Succulents and Spells
  Microscopes and Magic
  Alpaca and Apparitions
  Data and Divination
  Weddings and Witchcraft

Charley Deacon Series

Tides of Magic
  Tides of Change